Percy
AND THE KITE

by Christopher Awdry

illustrated by Ken Stott

Heinemann · London

William Heinemann Ltd
Michelin House
81 Fulham Road
London SW3 6RB
LONDON · MELBOURNE · AUCKLAND
First published in 1992
Copyright © William Heinemann Ltd 1992
0 434 96069 1
Printed in Great Britain by
Cambus Litho Ltd, East Kilbride

In a field beside Thomas's branch line a big tent was being
put up. Balloons and flags hung everywhere. A notice said:
GRAND KITE-FLYING COMPETITION – HERE TOMORROW.

"I want to fly a kite," said Percy.
"Engines don't fly kites," said Thomas. He remembered
what had happened when he went fishing.

Visitors came to the kite-flying competition from miles around. Thomas, Annie and Clarabel were kept very busy and Toby, Henrietta and Daisy helped too.

Percy was sad not to be able to help, but the Fat Controller had important work for him to do.

"My son, Jake, is flying a kite in the competition," said the foreman. "You watch for it – it's a special green one."

The big day was bright and sunny with a strong wind,
just the right weather for flying kites.

As Percy began work, the kites were racing into the sky.
Soon he spotted a big green one.

"That green one is flying well," said Percy's driver.
As they drew nearer, Percy thought he recognised it.
He was right – it was a green engine just like him.

"That must be Jake's kite," said his driver.
Percy was thrilled. "Peep, peep, it's me – I'm flying,"
he whistled happily.

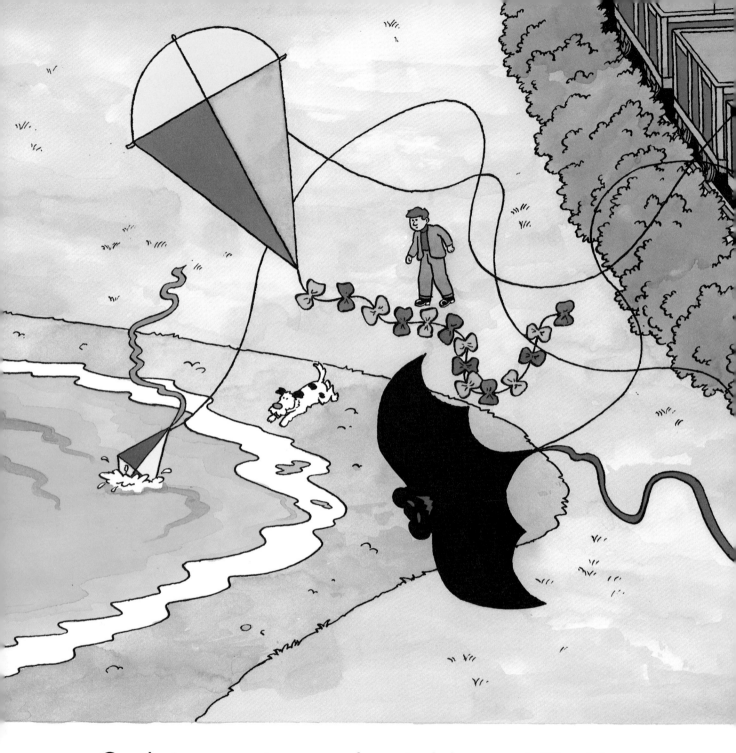

On their return journey the wind dropped. The kites began to dip and dive towards the ground. One even fell into the lake.

"What will happen now?" asked Percy anxiously.
"When the wind blows again it will soon carry them up,"
said his driver.

At the next station they met Thomas.
"Feeling hungry, Percy?" he called.

Percy was puzzled. "What does he mean?" he asked
his driver.
"I haven't a clue," replied the driver.

Toby was waiting at the top station.
"When does the party start, Percy?" he asked.

Percy's driver jumped down from the cab. He looked at Percy's funnel and burst out laughing.

"Well, well, Percy," he exclaimed. "You've been flying a kite without knowing it." He unwound a string from Percy's funnel and showed him a kite like an iced cake.

Percy laughed. "So that's what they meant by a party," he said. "I wish we could really eat that cake."

They took the cake kite back to the field on their next journey. They arrived just in time to see the First Prize being given to...

...Jake, for his ki
"I won, I won," w
better than flyi